P9-CAE-972

The Skull Talks Back

and Other Haunting Tales

The Skull
and Other

COLLECTED BY Zora Neale Hurston

ADAPTED BY Joyce Carol Thomas

Talks Back

Haunting Tales

ILLUSTRATED BY Leonard Jenkins

 HARPERCOLLINS*PUBLISHERS*

Sources as they appeared in *Every Tongue Got to Confess:*
Negro Folk-Tales from the Gulf States:

"Big, Bad Sixteen": Jerry Bennett. "Bill, the Talking Mule," "High Walker,"
"The Witch Who Could Slip Off Her Skin," "The Skull Talks Back," and
"The Haunted House": A.D. Frazier. Age 53. Barber. Georgia born.

Library of Congress Cataloging-in-Publication Data
Hurston, Zora Neale.
The skull talks back and other haunting tales / by Zora Neale Hurston ; adapted by
Joyce Carol Thomas ; illustrated by Leonard Jenkins.—1st ed. v.   cm.
Contents: Big, bad Sixteen—Bill, the talking mule—The skull talks back—The witch
who could slip off her skin—High Walker—The haunted house. Summary: Six haunting
stories collected by folklorist Zora Neale Hurston while doing field research in the Gulf
States in the 1930s. ISBN 0-06-000631-5 — ISBN 0-06-000634-X (lib. bdg.)
1. Children's stories, American. 2. Horror tales. [1. Horror stories. 2. Short stories.] I.
Thomas, Joyce Carol. II. Jenkins, Leonard, ill. III. Title.
PZ7.H95727 Sk 2004   2003022215   [Fic]—dc22

Typography by Martha Rago
1 2 3 4 5 6 7 8 9 10 ❖ First Edition

To Roy T. Thomas III
— J . C . T .

The Zora Neale Hurston Trust gratefully thanks
Joyce Carol Thomas and Leonard Jenkins for their superb work.
The Trust is also very thankful for the vision and guidance of
Susan Katz, Kate Jackson, and our wonderful editor, Phoebe Yeh.
Lastly, as always, our continued appreciation of Cathy Hemming
and Jane Friedman, who daily work tirelessly on behalf of Zora.

Contents

The Skull Talks Back

and Other Haunting Tales

Big, Bad Sixteen

YEARS AGO there was a man who wore size sixteen shoes. He was so big, fast, and strong they called him Big Sixteen.

One morning Big Sixteen said, "I think I'll go down to the pasture and catch me a wild hog."

"You're strong, but a wild hog's stronger than any man I know," said one of his friends.

Big Sixteen ran that hog down until he caught him.

"Didn't think you could do it," said his friend. "You just got lucky."

To prove it wasn't just luck, Big Sixteen thought he'd try something else to test his strength.

So the next morning, he wanted to put some new blocks under his house to keep it from falling down.

Since there were some huge twelve by twelves in the cow lot, he thought he'd go down and see if he could pick them up.

His friend said, "You need some help. You can't lift twelve by twelves all by yourself. They're too heavy!"

But Sixteen went on anyway and picked up a twelve by twelve on his shoulder, like it was a piece of straw.

He brought more twelve by twelves on back and used them to shore up the building.

The next morning, he decided to test his

strength again. He said, "I believe I'll go catch all the chickens in the farm yard."

"ALL the chickens? You can't. That's too many," his friend said.

Well, Big Sixteen caught all the chickens roosting in the yard *and* the trying-to-get-away chickens that flapped up and hid in the trees.

How many? Two thousand.

His friend said, "Big Sixteen, you're so strong and quick, I believe you can catch the Devil."

Big Sixteen said, "Yeah, I can catch him."

Next morning he thought about how he'd go catch the Devil. He said, "All right, I need a shovel and a big ten-pound sledgehammer."

Big Sixteen got the shovel and the hammer and walked out about two hundred yards in front of the house and commenced digging in the dirt—digging this hole.

Finally, he came to the Devil's house and knocked on the door.

The Devil's wife asked, "Who is it?"

He said, "Big Sixteen."

"What you want?"

"Is Jack the Devil here?" he asked.

"Yes."

"Tell him I want to see him."

The Devil cracked the door open and peeked out. Big Sixteen tapped him in the forehead with that hammer and killed him.

Then he ran and grabbed him up and carried him across his huge shoulder and back up to show him off to his buddies.

His buddies told him, "We don't want that ugly thing—take him back!"

Big Sixteen drug the Devil back and threw him in that same hole he had dug, covered him with dirt, and buried him.

About two weeks later, Big Sixteen died and he went to hell.

The Devil's children saw him coming, and

they took off running and hiding.

The Devil's wife saw him coming so straight 'til she slammed the door so hard, she scared herself.

Big Sixteen walked up and knocked on the door and she asked, "Who is it?"

"Big Sixteen," he said.

"Go 'way! Go back! We don't want you down here—you're too bad!"

Big Sixteen turned and went away. He marched on up to heaven.

When he got to heaven, he knocked on the pearly gates. They asked, "Who is it?"

"Big Sixteen," he said.

They said, "Go on 'way from here. We don't want you here—you're too bad!"

Well, there was no place else for Big Sixteen to go. So he had to come on back down to earth.

When he started falling back to earth, his soul changed into a ball of fire.

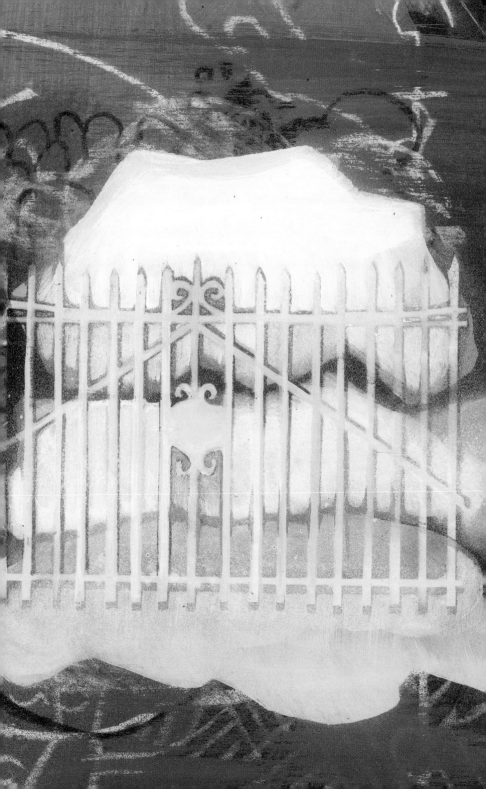

Even today, you can see him wandering

We call him Jack-o'-Lantern, but it's nobody
but Big Sixteen.

Bill, the Talking Mule

A FARMER had a mule named Bill.

He worked Bill every day, all day.

Mornings when the farmer went to fetch the mule, he'd say, "Come on 'round, Bill."

The farmer had a little feisty dog that he called Feist.

Feist trotted behind him everywhere he went.

One morning the farmer slept too late.

Feist did his duty—he barked until he woke the farmer up.

The farmer decided while he was drinking some coffee to send his son to go catch the mule.

"Go down there, boy, and bring me that mule up here."

The boy was fast, always running and doing things and not thinking very hard.

The farmer's son quickly grabbed the bridle and rushed lickety-split on down to the pasture to catch old Bill.

He said, "Come on 'round, Bill."

The mule looked around at the boy.

The boy told the mule, "Ain't no use you rolling your eyes at me. Pa wants you this morning. Come on 'round and stick your head in this here bridle."

The mule kept on looking at him, and finally said, "Every morning, it's, 'Come on 'round, Bill.' Every single morning, it's 'Come on 'round.' Why, I can't hardly get a good night's rest before somebody's calling, 'Come on 'round, Bill.'"

The boy's eyes got big as pie pans when the mule spoke.

He threw down that bridle and flew back to his house and told his pa, "Poppa, that mule's talking. Mule's talking. That mule's talking, I tell you!"

His father said, "Oh, go on away from here making up stories. Go on back down yonder and catch that mule!"

"No, Pa, that mule's done gone to talking, I tell you. I ain't going. You have to go catch Bill yourself."

The farmer looked at his wife and said, "See

what a big whopper that boy's telling? A talking mule! I declare!"

So the farmer, his feisty dog following on his heels, started out and went on down after the mule himself.

When the farmer and his dog got down to the pasture, he hollered, "Come on 'round, Bill."

The old mule looked around and said, "Every morning it's 'Come on 'round, Bill.'"

The farmer jerked his head up and then lit out with Feist right behind him.

He was huffing and puffing when he hit the door. He told his wife, "That boy told much the truth! That mule's talking up a storm. I never in all my born days heard a mule talk before."

The little feisty dog said, "Me neither. I got skeered."

That was the last straw. When the farmer heard even the dog talking, he took off running again.

Right through the woods he ran, with little Feist chasing behind him.

He ran so fast, he ran out of his shoes. He ran so fast, the wind got under his coat and that flew off too.

The dog panted and ran beside him in such a hurry his little legs trembled.

Way after while, the man stopped and tried to catch his breath.

He said, "I'm so tired I don't know what to do!"

His feisty dog sat down in front of him, wagged his worried tail, and said, "Me too."

The old man took off running again.

He nearly ran himself to death.

That man is still running to this day.

The Skull Talks Back

A LONG TIME AGO a man sold himself to the Devil.

He gave the Devil his whole soul and body to do with as the Devil pleased.

"Devil, you're the high chief," said the man as he walked out into this drift of woods.

He lay down flat on his back, in the middle of all these skull heads and bloody bones, thinking about how much he liked the Devil.

The Lord looked in on him.

The man said, "Go 'way, Lord."

"Why?" the Lord asked.

"Because," said the man, "I want to do everything in the world that's wrong and never do nothing that's right.

"Come here, Devil," said the man, "and do with me as you please."

And the Devil came to him.

The Devil whispered in his ear and told him lots of wrong things to do, like telling untruths. Stealing and cheating.

And just as the man promised, he obeyed the devil. He did everything wrong and nothing right.

The man dried up and died away on doing

wrong. His meat all left his bones and the bones got separated.

At that time High Walker walked upon the man's skull head and kicked the old skull head and kicked and kicked it on ahead of him many and many times.

He said to the skull head, "Rise up and shake yourself. High Walker is here!"

Old skull head wouldn't say a mumbling word.

Old skull head looked back over his shoulder, because he heard a noise behind him.

It was his Bloody Bones. Skull head said, "Bloody Bones, don't say nothing yet."

Then the skull said to High Walker, "My mouth brought me here, and if you don't mind, yours will bring you here."

Of course what the skull head meant was his telling everything he knew and bragging about him had caused his downfall.

But did High Walker listen? No.

High Walker went on back to his boss and

told him, "I saw a dry skull head talking in the drift today."

The boss said, "I don't believe it."

"Oh well, if you don't believe it, come go with me and I'll prove it. And if that skull head won't speak, you can chop my head off right where it's at."

So the boss man and High Walker went back in the drift to find this old dried-up skull head.

When High Walker walked up to the skull head, he began to kick and kick the old dried-up head, but it wouldn't say one word.

High Walker's boss thought High Walker had made the story up, so the boss cut High Walker's head off.

Then the old dry skull head said to High Walker, "See that now. I told you that mouth brought me here and if you didn't mind, it'd bring you here too."

So the Bloody Bones rose up and shook themselves, and the boss said, "What you mean by this?" He wanted to know what was going on.

Old skull head said, "We got High Walker and Bloody Bones. Now we're all three in the drift together."

The Witch Who Could Slip Off Her Skin

WAY OUT in the woods lived a witch woman who could get out of her skin, I mean step right out of her skin and go ride people she didn't like.

The witch woman had a saddle cat and a great big looking glass.

When she got ready to go out and ride her enemy, she'd take off all her clothes and lay them out. Stretch them out on a bed so she wouldn't have any trouble getting back in them when she rushed home. Then she'd slip out of her skin and lay it out next to her clothes.

When she and the cat were getting ready to go out, she went before the looking glass, shook herself, and said, "Slip 'em and slip 'em again!"

The old skin slipped off.

Now she could get mad at somebody for even the smallest thing. Once she rode a woman who gave her a red handkerchief instead of a white one.

She rode the woman until her legs gave out and the poor thing had to be wheeled around in a wheelchair.

Another time a man gave her polka-dot socks instead of striped ones. She rode him too. "Oh, my back hurt so bad," he moaned, until he couldn't lift his feet to get out of bed.

On this particular day after she slipped the old skin off, she started toward the door to ride her old boyfriend, the one who gave her red roses instead of lilies. She didn't like roses.

When she closed the door behind her, she looked back and said, "Umph! I forgot something." She wanted the skin to be warm when she came back in from riding.

She turned back to her house and blew through the keyhole and said, "Open the door, and let me come in again."

Once she and her saddle cat got in, she went and spread the old skin out by the fireplace and told the skin, "Remember who you are."

Now her old used-to-be boyfriend who used

to love her so hard and who had brought her the wrong color flowers was eavesdropping and spying on her.

When she left the house this time to go do him some harm, he slipped in her door and sprinkled her old skin with red pepper and white salt.

The witch woman couldn't find her used-to-be boyfriend at his house. "He's not here, so I can't ride him today," she said.

So she and her saddle cat made their way back home.

Her door wouldn't open. "Umph! I'm the witch woman, but I believe I've been locked out."

So she leaned over and blew through the keyhole, but the door got tighter.

She squinched her lips and blew again, saying, "Witchcraft, won't you let me in?"

Her old used-to-be boyfriend peeped from behind the house and watched her with a smile on his face.

She jiggled the knob until the door cracked open and she and her cat went in.

She looked around. Everything looked all right.

She said to the old skin, "Well, I'm tired. I believe I'll get back in my skin and go to bed."

When she put the old skin on, the old skin began to burn and sting. She laid it back down and looked at it.

She picked it up again and said, "Skin, oh skin, oh skin, don't you know me?"

She tried the skin on again, and it burned and stung her again. Worse this time.

She said, "Listen! Old skin, this is me. I've been going and going, and nothing like this has ever happened before. I do believe somebody conjured me. Must be my old used-to-be boyfriend, trying to keep me home."

Her old used-to-be boyfriend, speaking behind the house, said, "You used to have me, but I got you now."

High Walker

A MAN NAMED High Walker walked into a graveyard with skull heads and other bones strewn all around.

He called, "Rise up, Bloody Bones, and shake yourself."

And the bones would rise up and come together and shake themselves, then part and lay back down.

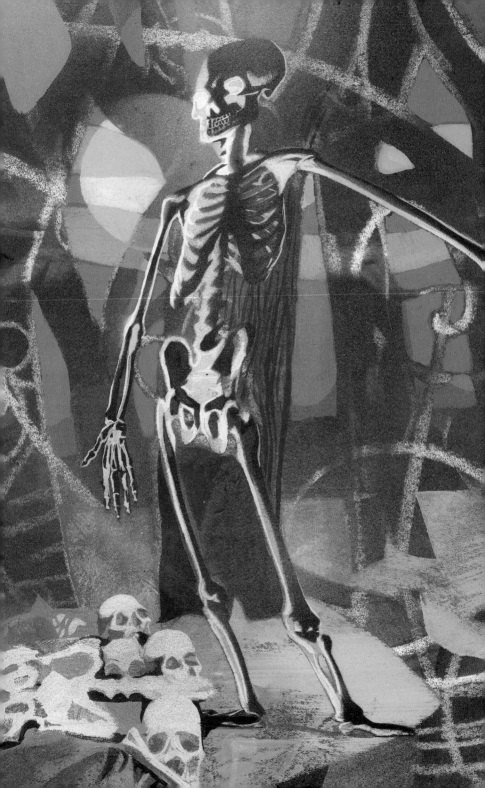

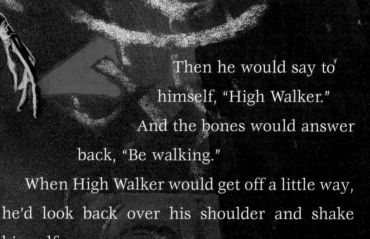

Then he would say to
himself, "High Walker."
And the bones would answer
back, "Be walking."
When High Walker would get off a little way,
he'd look back over his shoulder and shake
himself.
Then he'd say, "High Walker and Bloody
Bones."
The bones would shake themselves.
High Walker knew he had power.

The Haunted House

IN BULLARD COUNTY, Alabama, there was a haunted house and you had to spend the entire night so you could tell what happened during the wee hours.

There was guitar playing and songs, so the guests had music to console themselves.

Gamblers and preachers, drunkards and other dissipated classes had come to amuse one another and see what happened.

The first thing to come in at twelve o'clock was a big black cat, and he would come sit by the hearth with his back to the fire and his face to the guests.

Then for one hour the wind would blow and the lights would go out just as fast as you lit them.

So the guests would get scared and run out and they couldn't tell anybody anything about what happened in that house but this, "The black cat come in and the lights went out."

Some more guests came. The cat came in with them. Standing there with his back to the fire and his face to the people.

The guests began playing music. They intended to stay until day.

The wind began to blow, and all the lights went out again.

They stood the whole hour and the lights came back on.

Now when the wind rose, the door was already locked and thumb bolted. But it flew open.

In walked a pair of white feet.

The feet stood before the fire with their heels to the fire and their toes pointed to the people.

When the door opened again, the legs came in and joined the feet.

The door was still locked.

Next time the thighs came in and joined the legs.

Now when the door opened again, in came the body and joined onto the thighs.

Next time in came the arms and joined onto the body.

When the door opened again, the head came in and said, "Now, by God, we got the man."

The guests said, "No, by God, I don't know if you got the man or not. I know this—you got a run on your hands."

The people began to run so fast you couldn't see them.

Adapter's Note

IN THE STORY "Big, Bad Sixteen," the man Big Sixteen's oversized feet are so outrageous, they're scary. Big Sixteen outwits the Devil so thoroughly that when Big Sixteen dies, he has no place to go. He can't go to hell and he can't find a home in heaven. Even the angels lock the Pearly Gates when he tries to get in, terrified he'll attack one of them.

A mule gets weary of working in "Bill, the Talking Mule." That overworked mule talks back when pushed too far. Then everybody— the man, little Feist, and us—get to running "skeered."

High Walker is so fierce, he needs two stories. He stars in "The Skull Talks Back," as well as the tale carrying his name, "High Walker."

A Witch Woman slips in and out of her skin. She and the saddle cat and their eerie comings and goings make the hair stand up on our heads.

Another cat in "The Haunted House" raises the hackles on the backs of our necks. *Woo!* And those creepy feet without a body! Disconnected! Two feet standing by the hearth

with heels to the fire and the toes pointed
toward a room full of quaking folks!

Why do you suppose that in *The Skull Talks
Back* somebody's always running?

—JOYCE CAROL THOMAS

About Zora Neale Hurston

ZORA NEALE HURSTON was a celebrated anthropologist, folklorist, and novelist. While traveling in the rural South in the late 1930s, she collected stories from ordinary folk as part of her commitment to preserving and sharing their rich culture and oral traditions. In her groundbreaking novel *Their Eyes Were Watching God* and folklore collections in such important works as *Mules and Men, Dust Tracks on a Road,* and *Every Tongue Got to Confess,* Ms. Hurston redefined the clever wit, spirited character-ization, and distinctive voices she discovered. During a time when there were very few African-American and women writers, Ms. Hurston emerged as a literary pioneer.

Deemed a "cultural revolutionary" by Alice Walker and "our own walking, talking, swagger-ing history lesson" by Nikki Giovanni, Zora Neale Hurston has bequeathed a legacy to the literary community and beyond. Her books for children, including *What's the Hurry, Fox?* and *The Skull Talks Back,* will enlighten and entertain generations of new readers.

About Joyce Carol Thomas

JOYCE CAROL THOMAS is a playwright, poet, and National Book Award–winning author. She wrote MARKED BY FIRE and HOUSE OF LIGHT; the Coretta Scott King Honor Books BROWN HONEY IN BROOMWHEAT TEA and I HAVE HEARD OF A LAND; and GINGERBREAD DAYS, CROWNING GLORY, and THE GOSPEL CINDERELLA. Ms. Thomas lives in Berkeley, California. You can visit her online at www.joycecarolthomas.com.

About Leonard Jenkins

LEONARD JENKINS has garnered much attention, both nationally and internationally, for his bold, vibrant paintings, which have been exhibited in New York; Chicago; Philadelphia; Washington, D.C.; and Moret-sur-Loing, France. Mr. Jenkins's illustrations have added drama to I'VE SEEN THE PROMISED LAND and MALCOLM X, both written by Walter Dean Myers. Leonard Jenkins lives with his wife, Etta, in New York City and teaches at the Pratt Institute.